Poetic Transitions

WINTER

(THE 1ST OF A 4 PART SERIES)

Adesha L. Madison-Earl

authorHOUSE®

AuthorHouse™
1663 Liberty Drive
Bloomington, IN 47403
www.authorhouse.com
Phone: 1-800-839-8640

First published by AuthorHouse 10/6/2009

ISBN: 978-1-4389-9006-4 (sc)

Printed in the United States of America
Bloomington, Indiana

This book is printed on acid-free paper.

Eternal Dedication

Let it be understood, that if to no one else ANY and EVERY honorable and positive thing that I do, is dedicated to my ALMIGHTY Heavenly Father, God. He has blessed me with the talent that I have, and I must bless him by pursuing that talent and always giving him and his kingdom the praise.

Furthermore be it understood that everything I do is likewise ALWAYS in honor of certain individuals: Eddie Taylor, for sharing his love, life, and Christianity with me, and loving me as much as Jesus does.

To my children, Xavier, Chorlandrious, Christopher, and Keon, who have all made me feel that no matter how much I felt I lost in life; God has always compensated me with so much more. We have loved, laughed, and learned together. Thanks for helping me grow up.

To Janet W. Ward, OMG, there is not enough gratitude to express, there are no words to say, how many times you have saved my life in more than one way.

To my mom, Ruby Lee Madison, for serving her divine purpose in transporting me here. To my mother, Corine Taylor, for initiating this dream.

To my Godmother, Hattie Elizabeth Archie, for interceding after Aunt Corine's death, when I needed a family the most and mine gave up on me, gone but definitely, not forgotten.

To Aunt Lucille for attempting to be the mother to me that her sister did not live to be.

To my Aunt Lou Ella who always encouraged and believed in me, and for having been the happy and courageous soul that she was. She always gave me the true sense of an unfailing family. Unfortunately she left me before I could get this book in print; she is gone but DEFINITELY not forgotten!!!!

Contents

<u>Special Acknowledgement</u>

To my editor and new found friend, the inspirational Dr. Maxine Thompson, for including me in her hectic schedule, giving me an affordable rate, and promoting me via her radio show, words cannot describe the appreciation in my heart for all of this.

To Sarah Allen and Yvonne Reed, two strong, Christian, African-American women who were there for me when I needed someone the most and felt as if I had lost everything except my mind.

To Bertha Smith for one day reminding me of my dream and encouraging me to follow through with it.

To my cousin Zelda Hicks for being the strong and spiritual individual that she is. For not being afraid to step forward and take a chance on an unsure future when I relocated to Ohio. For believing in me, my children, and our future and participating in making it a brighter one.

To my mother-in-law Mrs. Lucille Carter for being a genuine Christian example that God will allow us to go through some things, but if we pray, believe, and live on, true spiritual compensation will come. It may not seem like it then, but it will come if we just believe, and for being the type of person that practices what she preaches.

To my Godmother Mrs. Ethel Mae Hines, she doesn't have any daughters, and I didn't have a mother. But, God has allowed us to have one another. I am thankful that she has always been honest with me, fair to me, and believed in and encouraged me.

To My Extra Special Step-Son, Henry Keith Earl, who is more like a son, than a step-son. There will never, in all the history of stepchildren, be another as wonderful or special as you. You are my #1 fan and I am yours, thanks for ALWAYS keeping it REAL!

To My Husband, Mr. Ronald Wayne Earl, who believed in me, even when I did not believe in myself. He encouraged me take my dreams off the shelf and put them here, furthermore, with him around, I will always have a poem.

<u>Blanket Acknowledgement</u>

To young African-American Divas that are definitely holding their own and setting great examples and moving forward no matter what: Mrs. Amanda S. Payton, Ms. Chawone "C.C." Ardrey, Ms. Myra Carter, and last but definitely not least, Ms. Kim (Keep It Moving) Penn. You all are a true inspiration for the discouraged.

To women who are a great inspiration to all of their following generations such as my role models: Dr. Maya Angelou, Oprah Winfrey, and Mrs. Michelle Obama.

To the men pioneers of the field that I hope my children and other young men will use as a role model such as Tyler Perry, Michael Baisden, Will Smith, and definitely President Obama.

To anyone that feels or knows that they have been a positive motivation and truly had my best interest and well-being at heart, it is not my intention to omit anyone. Thank you

"Poetic Transitions (Winter), Adesha L. Madison- Earl's first collection of poems, is an offering so wrought with poignancy and beauty that reading them will both exhilarate and exhaust you. A new talent on the scene, Adesha Madison-Earl is sure to go far in the world of poetry."

Dr. Maxine Thompson
<u>Black Butterfly Press</u>

A letter to my Father

Dear God,
To love is to be loved,
I thought the saying went.
Lately it seems as though
This is not how my time is spent.
I apologize, first of all,
For not praying like I should,
The devil had me strung so far along,
I had lost my faith for good.
Because of many family members' deaths,
And other relationships being buried as well,
My life has been nothing short of an emotional hell,
Now I seem to figure it has been as such,
Because I have not turned to your word as much.
And likewise another belief
Is that G-O-D still spells relief,
I was so worried about earthlings,
That I failed to bend a knee.
Until now, that was something about myself,
That I just couldn't see,
Confessions of all these things sometimes hurt
But, you're always there forgiving, and accepting them
For what they are worth.
Thank You for what you are allowing me to do,
Correct my life before it is ruined.
Forgive me, I pray, for treating you this way.
If you accept my apology, I promise not to stray.
In Jesus Name,
Amen

<u>A Psalm for Mothers</u>

Lord on high, God up above,

Help me to learn and to love.

Help me to be a good influence in my child's life.

Strengthen me to endure through misery and strife.

Give me the ability to give appropriate advice and to share,

Teach me how to be patient and teach me how to care.

Help me teach them to stand up for right.

Help me to teach them with Jesus there is no battle impossible to fight.

Last, but not least, help me remember to pray each day

That I may live by example, and not fall too far along the way.

<u>A Friend</u>

A friend is one, who listens and finds ways to understand,
They're good at giving advice and knowing when not to demand.
They're not only there through the good times,
But also in times of hurt,
They'll stand by your side to help achieve your goals,
And ensure that your dreams work.
They encourage, rather than insult,
Gesture after gesture brings good results.
They are always glad to assist,
Always there with a smile,
This is the genuine personality that makes friendship more worthwhile.
They make life more interesting to live,
They make gifts more fascinating to give,
They feel that you are special,
When you can't see how that is true,
This person sees all the unique qualities within you.
This is the definition of a friend's characteristics,
From what I can plainly see,
This is someone I would like to entertain the opportunity
Of having a friendship with me!

<u>A Friendly Betrayal</u>

They say they care,
They really don't.
They claim they will do things
They really won't.
Good friends are they
When money is fine,
Other than that
They just insist on lying.
"I'm your friend and am always near,"
Is their quote,
But when times become difficult
They're up in smoke.
"I love you and will never stray,"
I've been told.
Yet when negative situations arise
That grows old.
"I'm not a fair-weather friend,"
They declare again and again,
When trouble comes
Where are they then?
I hear that same tired old line,
"I'll love you forever,
Dear friend of mine."
These are falsehoods
That I've learned not to trust.
When I do, my dreams turn into dust.
I had a friend, who told me things as such,
I trusted her long enough to find out that she talked too much.
The secrets I told her she sang out like a song,
Despite the fact that she knew it was wrong.
I told her things in seriousness
And she laughed in my face,
Now she acts as if she has never met me at all.
She ignores me to the fullest up and down the school halls

She hangs with her buddies and so-called friends,

I am the farthest thing from her mind then.

When they laugh and it's me they scorn,

I continuously smile though my heart has been torn.

She doesn't seem to be concerned,

Seems to me, she doesn't give a darn,

Until problems arise in her life.

She comes to me and I treat her nice,

I try my best to listen and to be a good friend

Though she's not right with me

I have an ear to lend.

The Best Friend in the world,

I know is not me.

But, with the help of God, I try to be.

I don't intend to backbite,

I don't intend to try,

Not look into your eyes and tell a lie.

I will not hurt you intentionally,

I will try to always tell the truth,

I'm willing to listen if you're feeling down and blue

I'm looking at the woman in the mirror,

And I think it's time for a change,

From this day forward,

A faithful friend I will remain,

Even though everyone continues to hurt me,

A loyal friend I will constantly be.

No matter how hard I try in life,

People's negativity cuts like a knife.

I believe in my soul and heart,

This is A Friendly Betrayal

Because we both played the part!

<u>**Again**</u>

Tears stream like a flowing sea

Emotions have become more serious

Than I ever thought they would be.

I am in a position I never thought I'd see

I use to think "heart broken"

Was just a word or two

Now the thought no longer seems absurd

Seems more like it's true.

In past times it seemed easy to love,

Show my feelings, and show that I care

Presently I tend to feel it's easier

Pretending that I'm not there.

Expressing my concerns and telling my thoughts at will

Only gets me mistreated, and makes me feel lowly and unreal

Mistakes have been made,

But never have amends

When I think everything's all right

It only starts over again.

Is it best to walk away, and never look back?

Is it best to try a new start and handle it with care and tact?

Should I try or should I give up?

Will it be worth it or is it pressing my luck?

Why me?

Why now?

Why all of this?

Is this the beginning of a new life or only death's kiss?

Maybe they told me,

Maybe they tried,

Maybe facts I overlooked

And the truth I denied.

Now I have a child

And one on the way,

Is it too late?

Is it a new start as of this day?

Why do I feel like this again, year after year?
Am I really living, or am I only lingering here?

<u>An Answered Prayer</u>

Night after dark and lonely night,
I dried tear after painful tear,
No one was with me
To gently hold me near.
Friend after so-called friend
Turned their deceiving backs,
Leaving nothing but burdensome memories behind
Of life's trodden tracks.
Some memories of family are positive,
Majority of them are not,
They always refresh my memory
Of all that I haven't got.
I prayed a special prayer
And hoped that you would hear,
You gave me a remarkable answer
My son, full of life and cheer.
Filled with smiles and laughter
And sweet sincerity,
In him I have found
Earthly prosperity,
He is enough to soothe my soul
And more than the satisfaction for which I longed,
Knowing he is alive and well,
My day can never go wrong.
My prayers have been answered,
My needs were compassionately heard,
Thank you for your son, Jesus Christ,
And for your Holy Word.

Written in dedication to my 3rd born son Christopher Edward Reese Earl

A Psalm for Christians

Dear Father in Heaven,

Lord up above,

Please bless me with

Patience, compassion, and love.

And besides those things,

Strength and wisdom, too,

So that I, Dear Jesus,

May live for you.

Please do not let me take my blessings for granted,

But, accept them with all of my heart.

Please let me not worry about others

But, worry about whether or not I am doing my part.

Let my life be of a great influence to another

That they may become a Christian sister or brother,

Let me remember to put you first and pray each day

So that I may remain a Christian faithfully and not go astray.

A Valentine Lyric

Never before have I felt as good
As I feel inside right now,
You are the reason I feel this way,
You did this to me and I don't know how.
You came to me for a reason,
And definitely when I needed someone,
You came to me with understanding,
And stopped the chase my heart was on.
You have shown a genuine compassion
That can only come from the soul,
You have given me the gift of laughter,
Warming a personality that once was cold.
You have shown consideration in ways
Words cannot describe
You have given me something to look forward to,
With an anticipation that I cannot hide.
Your actions have spoken louder than your words,
You were proven to be true,
This poem has been written as an expression of love,
From all of me, especially for all of you.

Daddy

Why help bring a child into the world,
_ If you don't want it?_
To have that child growing up,
Feeling teased and taunted,
To lead that child on,
Making her believe that you care,
She gets the impression she's wrong,
Because you are never there.
When she needs money for school
_ Or other financial matters,_
All you do is fib and throw lame excuses at her.
On special occasions, or everyday
Where are you?
When she's in the hospital or feeling blue?
It's pathetic when you don't show
For your own daughter's birth,
This portrays one of the most ridiculous men on earth,
To give her a little spending change
And smile once in a while,
That's not helping the little girl live,
Nor is it rearing the child,
You've denied your responsibility
_ And fatherhood._
You've avoided doing as much
As you possibly could.
When I grow up and become a big success
You will claim me then
Because I am one of the best.
It'll be too late;
I'll forgive and forget,
But you'll see what you were missing,
When your child you could have been with.

<u>Distinguishment</u>

It is the natural mom that actually gives birth,

Mother helps you realize

The reasons you are here on earth

A mother is the one there when needed,

She gives from the heart and is never greedy.

She makes sure her child has food before eating a bite

If her child's in trouble, she's ready to help fight.

She teaches her child the values of life and to go the right way,

She helps the child grow in Jesus and prays for it every day.

She loves her child and cherishes it, and helps it to do its best,

She stands by the child and encourages it, through every trial and test,

A mother's heart is sensitive and adheres to all needs,

She's good at giving advice and is full of kind deeds,

She teaches you that you are special, because you are God's child.

She makes you feel loved and lets you know that life is worthwhile.

She hurts when you hurt and cries when she sees your tears.

She's there to make you smile when you're down and calms every fear.

A mother has such a warm personality; it makes you feel secure,

When you're in her presence, you feel there's nothing you can't endure,

She's there when you feel you're unloved or no one cares.

She's teaches you to be assertive and in your problems she shares,

When you're ill and not feeling so swell,

She's there to lend a gentle touch and help until you're well.

She teaches that every person that smiles is not necessarily your friend,

"Yet and still," she says, "treat them right, and pray for them, even then."

A mom can be anyone able to conceive,

It takes a mother whose attention the child can receive.

It has been proven through time that neither a mom or another

Can live up to the distinguished characteristics of the person thought of as a mother.

Written in dedication to my Aunt Corine Wesley Taylor who was the only mother I had ever known from birth
until the age of fourteen

Distinguishment 2

Dad can be anyone that helps bring a child into the world,

Father is the one that takes care of that little boy or girl.

Dad can brag and think that he is a man, calling the child his own,

Father is the one who comforts the child when it feels all alone.

Dad can kiss the child on the forehead and say, "It will be all right."

Father stays there until the sickness is cured and out of sight.

Dad holds that child tight, but puts it down when it cries,

Father helps soothe the soul and wipes tears from the child's eyes.

Dad is there sometimes when he can fit it into his plan,

Father is there to be that strong, understanding, and patient man.

When people observe the good in the child, Dad notices a little more.

But Father is around in the midst of problems galore.

Don't misunderstand: all dads aren't the same,

But, a Father distinguishes himself by more than just a name!

Written in dedication to my Father, Eddie Taylor the only man that has ever loved me just as much as God!

Don't Go

I love you, Mother of mine,

Please allow me a little more time.

I cannot bear this hardship alone,

I know you have got to travel your pathway home.

I cannot withstand these trials and strife,

This world is cruel and burdens are not light.

You are the one, who helped ease the pain,

You have helped me, my self-confidence to gain.

You helped me, my true self to see,

You made me want to be all I can, just for me.

You encouraged me to never give up,

You helped me when things got rough.

You are the only one who will ever love me like that.

The rest have run instead of facing the facts.

No one cares besides you and my father,

They only think of themselves, they refuse to be bothered.

Please don't go!

I need you to stay,

I need another chance to prove how much I love you today,

So, I beg you with all of my heart,

Please Don't Go!

I can't stand to see you part.

Written in dedication to my mother, Aunt Corine shortly after her death

14

Emotionally Yours

When times got hard,

As they sometimes did,

Good advice you gave,

Your feelings you never hid.

When others acted mean and rude,

You opened the way to compassion,

And you weren't ever crude.

When others became irrational and acted out in haste,

In my life you found a special place.

When problems were overbearing,

I had no choice but to cry,

It was your caring smile that wiped tears from my eyes.

Sometimes I felt no one cared, or even gave a darn,

Yet you grew stronger in loyalty, and about friendship helped me learn.

Sometimes I wasn't sure if things were going to be okay or not,

Yet day after day, you grew as solid as a rock.

When others let me down, and talked behind my back.

You never failed that test, and did not give any slack,

When I'd lost all faith, hope for love, and respect,

You understood me and my opinions helped me check.

When I disappointed you or hurt you to your heart,

After accepting my apology, you offered a new start.

You do not fit anyone else's criteria; you're distinguished all by yourself.

I shall always be emotionally yours, because you

Have nurtured my emotional health!

This poem is a dedication to my cousin, and the Godmother of Keon Jayverick Deshawn Earl, Mrs. Isabella Denise Taylor Freeman. Thanks for being there for some of the times I needed someone most.

Feeling Misunderstood

No one loves me,

No one cares,

I have no one,

With which to share.

Every time I think I have a friend,

I have to sit down and think again.

I'm always the one hit in the back

By all of the "woodchoppers" with their axes.

I feel I'm good for nothing,

Because of how I'm treated I feel as cheap as dirt,

No matter how hard I try,

I always wind up hurt.

I try not to say anything,

I try to be a good friend,

But, the tears always come back again.

No matter how good,

No matter how bad,

By all of these folks,

I've been had.

They use me like a dog,

Except a few,

How would you feel

If they did it to you?

If they laughed in your face

When you tell problems you have,

But for pleasurable times,

They're always there

"Fair-weather friends" they're called (I think),

I don't care,

They all stink.

With your feelings

You attempt to be true,

They only mock and laugh at you.

They laugh at my clothing

And ridicule my name,
They beat me down into disgrace and shame.
My overweight body they make fun of
Yet they proclaim to have true love.
Why do they constantly lie?
Every night I have to cry.
Death is what I really want,
Not this life filled with taunt,
Hate comes in straight lines,
I have no friend to call all mine.
I find an "associate" I assume to be swell,
And some of my secrets I start to tell.
But like a chorus singing high,
They shout it out to the sky.
Singing loud and crystal clear,
They squeal it for the entire world to hear.
It seems impossible for people
To accept me as a shining star,
Though this is how it has been so far....
I pray to God it won't continue to be so hard.

Food for Thought

When life overwhelms you to the point of distress,

When your mind is focused on discouragement and everything less,

When your heart is so sorrow-filled all it can do is weep,

When your soul feels completely numb, as if it were asleep,

When your spirit is wandering as if it were a stranger in a foreign place,

When you have become so hate-filled and resentful

You cannot show God your face,

When depression is taking over, and your head is hung low,

When you've tried with all of your being,

And gone as far as you can go,

When all of these things occur and begin to set in,

When everyone's let you down and that includes your best friend,

But God is there for you, regardless of your doubt.

When He continues to restore his love, and never lets you go without,

This is when it should become apparent,

That he will never let you down,

This should give you the desire to share your love with Him,

From birth until you are buried underground.

For a Special Graduate

God fearing. As long as you have a special respect and fear in your heart for our Almighty Father, you will stay on the straight and narrow.

Respect. Maintain respect for yourself and others will have no option except to respect you. Be respectful and become respected.

Atttitude. Always maintain a positive attitude. The positivity that you carry within yourself will be displayed in the work you do, and will be felt when you are in the presence of others.

Drive. Never lose your drive. Always find a special motivation within yourself. Think of something or some things that were negative that happened to you and do everything in your power to ensure that the same thing never happens again, therefore maintaining your drive or determination.

Understanding. In order to acquire a good understanding, you have got to be willing to listen. But, do not listen with your physical ears; hear what goes on in the world around you.

Achievements. You have many accomplishments. Look how far you have come! Look at all the obstacles you had to hurdle to get where you are. Do not allow anyone to subtract from your success!

Triumphs! Allow your trials or tribulations to become your testimony!

Expendable. There is always an exception to every rule. Allow yourself the opportunity to be flexible and acceptable to change. Always compose a back-up plan, and you will be an <u>exceptional</u> person. There is no exchange for you, so don't ever sell yourself short.

<u>Congratulations Graduate!!!</u>

This poem was written as a special tribute to a young lady who is also now one of my stepdaughters, Twyla Earl, for her high-school graduation.

For the Love of My Life

For the times you strengthened me, and helped me make it through.

For the times you gave me encouragement, when I didn't know what to do,

For the times you gave me advice and made my life better to live,

For the times you didn't have much, but gave me what you did have to give.

For the times you believed in me and forgave me for doing wrong,

For the times you could've dismissed me, but you kept hanging on,

For the times you loved me when the situation looked bad,

For the times you seemed to be my only friend when inside I felt sad.

For the times you defended me when no one else seemed to care,

For the times you could have easily strayed but you chose to stay right there.

For the times I offended you and said things that were very mean,

For the times you overlooked it and kept your senses keen.

For the times I allowed time to pass and used it all in vain,

For the times you put aside your anger from my acting insane,

For the times you desired to do for me deep within yourself,

For the times you didn't give up on getting what I wanted but you needed a little help,

For all of the times you have given me yourself and sometimes more,

Those are the reasons why loving you should be an easy chore.

Those are the reasons why I shouldn't be ashamed and show too much pride,

Those are the reasons why I should let go of all the love I have inside.

Those are the reasons why making you happy should be my only task,

So now that I've finally found the true reasons, you no longer have to ask.

For you Big Mama

When one so precious enters our lives,
We do not wish to think of their leave,
And although we know maybe we should not,
All we can do is grieve.
The Bible tells us not to mourn
When a loved one is gone on,
For if they were saved we do know,
They are on their way home.
Hold your head up high,
Wipe all of the tears of pain away,
And try to see this clear,
She is doing better there
Than we are doing down here.
Everything she did
Shall be remembered well.
Each one of us
With special memories to tell.
The laughter,
The way she smiled with sentiment and glee,
The comforting words,
The food for thought,
For us she did leave.
The giving of her time
To family, to friends,
And to the community, one and all,
The way she made us feel good
When we were feeling kind of small.
A special place within our hearts
She will always hold,
A loving memory placed within our minds,
That will never grow old.
You are courageous, Big Mama,
You crossed the path we all must go,
You are loved, Big Mama,

And this we wanted you to know.

No more will you have to suffer

Any pain you may have gone through,

It is your time to rest in peace

And that is what we want you to do.

Written in dedication to my children's great grandmother Mrs. Katherine Jenkins Glover On behalf of Xavier and
Chorlandrious with love

__Friendship Means the World to Me__

If the world in its entirety were meaningless
And no concerned friend to be found,
If there wasn't any hope for tomorrow,
No way up, only heads held down.
If there were no words of wisdom from the elderly,
No way to pass the heritage on through an unborn child,
If we only lingered helplessly through the earth,
Lost and confused the whole while.
If we were left to make it alone
Through this treacherous and evil day,
If there wasn't anyone around
To help us proclaim a new way.
If we meant nothing to anyone
And love was eternally unreal,
If we only existed negatively
And didn't know how to "feel,"
The world would be our emotional prison,
Without a question or a doubt,
But, the only "if" we need be concerned with
And cannot live without,
Is if we live spiritually, we will meet "The Supreme and Holy One."
For now it's comforting to know,
Friends help us through our trials, one by one.

Godmother's Letter

G   *Goodness*

O   *"Omega"—*end*—of this there is none*

D   *Divine*

M   *Mercy*

O   *Of Which*

T   *there*

H   *has to be*

E   *eternal*

R   *rewards*

God always knows what is best for us,

In each situation he wants us, to in him put our trust.

If anyone would have told me

You would have been this close to me,

I would have probably said

That was something I could not see.

Throughout my sadness and gloom

You were there to see me through,

When the clouds moved over to reveal the sun

I looked and the first person I was you.

You were there to encourage me

Toward the right direction

You were there to renew my faith

With your love and affection.

What you have done for me

Can not and will not go unattended,

Your friendship has been genuine

And you have not pretended.

Characteristics of a God-driven person,

These are no other than,

Thanks for everything,

May the Lord bless you again and again,

Love you like a mother,

Adesha

Written for my Godmother, Mrs. Hattie Elizabeth Archie, (before she passed away), whom I remember more than my natural mother because she shared most of my life. Gone but not forgotten. Though we had our ups and downs, we had more ups than downs, and more understandings, than misunderstandings.

__Hard Times__

When times get hard and they sometimes will,

And the struggle you're in, seems all uphill,

It seems that you want to simply give up

Because the road has gotten a little rough.

Everyone goes their separate ways

And leave you in a puzzled gaze,

No one seems to give a care,

And in your problems,

They want no share.

Everyone is on your case,

Of true love, you can find no trace,

But, don't give up because things are hard,

Just lift your eyes and look to the Lord.

He has been there, and always will.

Yes, even when your battle seems all uphill.

He will be there no matter what the time,

That is why He is a good friend of mine.

Besides having the Lord Jesus, you have me.

So I am your true friend, too, you see,

I will not abandon you, when times get rough,

I'll always be there when times get tough.

When you think no one else is around,

I will always be somewhere to be found,

Right there after you talk to Jesus, you see,

Sit down for a while and talk to me.

I really and honest-to-God do care,

In your problems, I am glad to share.

That is the kind of friend, to you, I would like to be.

That is the kind of friend I would want you to be to me.

I love you with all of my heart and soul,

We will be sisters forever, and one as a whole.

This poem was written in high school, in dedication to who was then my best friend, Anita Turner, before we got separated in more than one way.

I am who I am

I am who I am,
I am who I would like to be.
I am all of the things in my appearance,
I am the things that go unseen,
I am what helps to make the world,
I am part of what it revolves around,
I am a person just like you,
So be a better person than to put me down,
I am a human being,
My feelings often change,
I am a complex child
And
I have a high emotional range.
I am who I am,
Not who you would like for me to be!
So accept me for who I am,
If you won't, I don't give a damn.

If I could

If I could grieve for you today,
I would.
If I could take your pain away,
I would.
If I could take on the feeling you had
When this news you heard,
If I could alleviate the heartache
That came from those aching words.
If I could take a Kleenex
And eternally wipe tears from your face,
If I could take a pencil
And this one confusing thing erase,
If I could give a simple remedy,
An over-the-counter relief,
If I could write a prescription:
"Take this once in a lifetime for grief"
If I could subtract all the feeling of loss,
If I could divide the sadness at all cost,

                                  I would.

But, this is unrealistic,
I know that I cannot,
So what I have to do
Is deal with what I have got.
I have got the ability to remind you
Of your family and your friends.
I can help you realize,
This is where it all begins.
Begins to be a new journey with Jesus,
For her and for you also,
For where she has been,
Where she has gone,
You are yet trying to go.
We don't have to wish her pain away,
For it is already gone,

We don't have to sit and wonder,
If she will safely make it home,
When God issued life,
His map and instructions were clear.
Do not get too comfortable
Because you will not be staying here,
You can stay for as long as I need
The mission carried through.
After that
When the time has come
I will send for you.
He sent for her,
She was ready to go,
And was taken with loving care,
Don't be fretful or mourn too long,
She will see you when you arrive there!

This poem was written as a dedication to Ms. Zola Freeman, the God Grandmother of my fourth son, Keon. This was the mother of his Godfather Mr. Steven Freeman.

I Wanted

I wanted to change myself for you,

I wanted to do something to make you be true.

I wanted to give more than I had given in the past,

I felt maybe that would make you appreciate what you have.

I wanted to make your world comfortable and worry-free,

I wanted your happiness so much that I forgot about me.

I wanted to build a life with you, not for you to move on,

I wanted us to make it work for our children,

 But you wanted to move along.

I wanted a life, not built from past accumulations,

But from fresh new starts,

I wanted us to be a consolation to one another

And to help mend each other's heart.

Evidently you wanted a source of convenience,

Not to help make a new way,

Not to ever have a problem,

Or go through anything, because you did not stay.

You knew what your goals and dreams were,

And that it didn't include me,

So why did you waste my time?

Using me to get to the place you wanted to be.

Materialistically, I lost nothing, but gained much more,

Time I cannot reacquire, that fact sits as an open sore.

Financially I broke even, but my emotions are torn,

Between my beautiful children I have to face each day,

And a love that evidently wasn't mine, which I now mourn.

<u>*Just Because*</u>

Just because you were a father,

And once held your children in your arms,

Just because you were a grandfather,

And once watched your "grands" play along.

Just because you were a brother,

And once brought a smile and wiped a tear,

Just because you were an uncle,

And once assured us you were here.

Just because you were a friend,

And helped out if you could,

Just because you were born,

You passed away as we knew you would.

Just because you suffered,

One day it had to end,

Just because God promised,

One day we will see you again.

This poem was written in dedication to my late Uncle L.C. Taylor with love

<u>**Justification**</u>

It is very hard to, in this world; find a true and loyal friend:

Someone with all of the major characteristics; compassion, concern, respect, generosity, humor, and devotion.

But, once in a lifetime you might get the chance

To meet that special someone,

Who shares the same morals and standards,

Who values friendship the way you do.

Someone forgiving and very trustworthy.

When we are privileged enough to have this happen,

It is like a dream, an unrealistic happening.

At one point in time, it may get so frightening

That you tend to have abnormal reactions,

Which causes that person to get hurt.

Not intentionally doing it,

But it's just that when you meet someone as such,

We don't know what to do.

But, Thank God they stay with us anyway.

This poem was written in dedication to my best friend, who later in life, I found out was my cousin, Shirley Mae Chambers, (though we have always claimed one another as God Sisters!).

Life is the Best Teacher

When I was five, my mom died,

I didn't know what was happening,

So I couldn't have cried.

When I started school,

I learned the basic death rule,

No one said, "Adesha, dear,

You mom's never going to be there—

When you get home from school,

And other children have treated you rude,

To be there when you cry,

And make you want to try,

Or on all those rainy days,

To stay in with you,

And find fun games to play."

My dad doesn't care

Whether I live or die,

Deep within that is painful,

But, I try not to cry.

Then I sit back and dream,

"Why do people do these things?"

"Why can't they love me for me?"

Not for what I wear,

But, for my qualities, oh so rare,

And be a friend so true,

The kind that is dedicated to you.

No one really attempts to love,

No one really makes an effort to care,

Though they don't desire a friend

With whom they can share.

I will exchange these negative thoughts for a hug,

An extremely meaningful one filled with lots of love.

So after this occurs, God will call my name,

Then peace and happiness shall reign,

I will be there and I will tell you why,

We need to work together to brighten the sky,
Remove the rain and allow the sun to shine in,
After a while, we will have a rainbow again.
SO……………………………………..
I don't care if no one loves me,
I don't care if no one cares,
That is their loss, you see.
They lost out on a good thing,
When they passed up the opportunity to get to know me!

<u>*Love*</u>

Love isn't something that can be bought or sold,

It is an emotion that deep within your heart you hold.

It takes time to develop and sometimes much time to grow,

But, when it comes into your life, you will be the first to know.

It will make you feel happy when you think that you are sad,

Instead of being angry, it causes you to feel glad.

When you are feeling down, depressed, and low,

It helps you to, in yourself, find that inner glow.

When you feel deserted, it helps you forget your sorrows,

It gives you joy and a sense of hope for a new tomorrow.

Sometimes it is hard for us to love, but we really want to,

The only thing we ask is for a friend ever so true.

Miracles

God gave you many miracles on the day you were born,

He gave you the senses he thought that you should have,

He gave you a reason and purpose for arriving here,

He gave you a chance at life in John 3:16,

An opportunity to live, learn, love and be somebody special enough that maybe,

At least one thing you do will be a positive influence on others,

He gave you a precious and creative expression to be the one and only exactly like you,

To fortify your world, he gave you a mother.

Not necessarily your birth mother, but a mother.

To care for you, share in, and strengthen your existence,

Don't take for granted the Miracles God gave you

Because when you take your Miracles for granted, you lose them.

Mother to All

When you are there to help every child in the neighborhood,

And you do everything that you could and should,

When you make a large sacrifice

And give up certain unneeded joys,

To help guide and teach each girl and every boy,

When you're there when things get rough,

To help create smiles and maintain laughs

And to redirect (if possible) someone who has fallen off the path,

To attend church every time you can, live, grow, and learn,

And to be worthy of the respect that you've gotten

Because it has been well-earned,

Then you know that your accomplishments have really gone far.

This is classified as a mother to us all, our bright and shining star.

<u>Mr.</u>

Child:

Why do you lie on the street, Mr.?

Are you here all alone?

Don't you have a house to go to?

Is this box your home?

Are these your things in this buggy?

Don't you have a closet or a room?

Do you have food to eat?

Do you lie here hungry, sad, and in gloom?

Do you have a family to give you love and care?

Don't you even have a friend, to show compassion and with whom to share?

Why do you look so ragged, dirty, tired, and worn?

Was it your choice to live like this?

Has your heart been torn?

Do you have clean water so that you may take a bath?

Do you bathe in the ditch water that leads the sewage path?

What will you do when it storms and you have no place to go?

Will you just sit in the rain until you are soaked?

Don't people mock you and laugh in your face?

Do they give you a chance because of your "race"?

Homeless person:

I lay here on the street, my child, because I belong.

No, I wouldn't be here if I had a place to call home.

No, I haven't a closet.

Yes, these things are mine.

I gather what I can from things people leave behind.

I have no decent food to eat.

I eat from the garbage can.

People walk over me, and regard me as a dirty old man.

If only I did have a family to give me some love and care,

My children would love me as their father,

As a friend, their lives I would share.

No, it wasn't my choice to live like this.

I should think not, my love.

The rain water is all that I have to bathe in, that God sends from above.

People will talk no matter where or who we are.

On my heart, they sometimes carve a shallow scar.

Do not take your blessings lightly.

Thank God every day.

Pray, work hard, and do your best.

Then you will not live this way.

This I leave with you, my child,

Not to worry about me please.

One day I will be with my heavenly father,

Beyond the nightly stars you see.

**My First Love**

As he places a moon in the sky
To illuminate the heavens at night,
As the stars creep from an unknown world
And radiate their beautiful light,
As the rain showers from the clouds above
And help produce new life in the ground,
As the birds soar through the air
And awake us with their hypnotizing sounds,
As the flowers gradually bloom,
Holding a special attraction for the eye,
As the deep blue ocean waves and currents
Caress the shores where they lie,
When the sun rises in the morning
And its lovely light is reflected upon the earth,
When the day is overflowing with touching moments,
Each with its own individual worth,
When my soul feels discouraged,
And my spirit is completely bound,
When I can be at peace all the while,
Knowing that joy has been found,
That is when I know my "love" understands.
I make mistakes
But, no matter what faults I may have,
"He" never displays hate.
I know He will be my comforter
When I am confused and feeling afraid.
I know that He will always catch my hand and guide me
Whenever I may stray.
I know He will be my rainbow
After many stormy days.
I know He will cradle my soul on all of those cold and lonely nights.
I know He will be my strength with I am weak.
And forgive me when I'm not right,
It is when I partake of natural beauties,

Such as those of an angel-like dove,
I remember why I am attracted to God,
My first real and true love.

This poem is especially dedicated to God, my father, my creator, the lover of my soul, definitely my ALL!

My Mom

A child was born,

Ignorant of the world,

It needed guidance,

It was conceived out of lust, want, and greed—

Man's basic downfall.

A woman had that child,

Being ignorant of motherhood.

She needed guidance,

For she was merely tasting the sting of,

Circumstantial consequences of life.

She knew not how to care for it.

Of love, she knew not,

Of responsibility, she wasn't aware,

She was "dumb" when it narrowed down to the child.

She was confused.

She was unsure of herself.

Her feelings or the basic needs of her own,

A man (the woman thought she loved),

Was in want,

He filled the woman's ears with the

Sweet sensation of words she desired to hear,

And the child was conceived

After the child entered the world.

Responsibility was not ready to be taken on by the woman (or the man),

A relative cared for the child,

As if it were her own,

The woman who gave birth to the child,

Checked on it every now and then,

For about five years, two months, nine days, but never really got acquainted with the child.

After the child turned five, the woman's last lust for worldly pleasures offered her a cup of death.

She left the child she had never gotten to know.

<u>Neglected</u>

When I was five, my mom died and left me all alone.

My aunt felt compassion for me

And turned her house into a home.

As life went on, it got a little better each day,

We became a strong family

In a special and loving way.

We were unaware and didn't expect the unexpected,

Our feelings were true, deep, hidden, and well-protected.

Then one day while I was at school, happy, and on the roam,

My mother fell: She had a heart-attack at home.

Maybe it was my fault—in a way—I was the blame;

Because of my personal problems,

She felt lots of sorrow and pain.

Seems like each time I get close to someone they have to leave

And I am left yet once again, to sit alone in agony and to grieve.

Orientation into Motherhood

I never became a beauty queen,

My curls wouldn't hold tight,

I never became an astronomer,

I only wanted to sleep at night.

I never became a singer,

I couldn't hold a note with a prayer,

I never became a scientist,

The love for formulas wasn't there.

I never became a mechanic,

I never was interested in fixing cars,

I never became an actress,

I didn't have to be the star,

I never became a teacher,

There were so many things I needed to know,

I never became a fashion designer,

I never did learn how to sew.

I never became an astronaut,

I had no desire to personally see the moon.

I never became a florist.

My flowers never would bloom.

I never became a farmer,

I bought my vegetables from the store,

I never became a counselor,

I always had problems and problems galore.

I never did anything extravagant,

Nothing that anyone couldn't have done,

I was blessed to proudly do what some have not,

The day God blessed me with my first son.

Written in dedication of the birth of my first born son, Clifton DalJuan Xavier Henry

Questioning Myself

There was a time I loved you,
Couldn't imagine myself without,
Lately it seems a feeling has overcome me
Of great suspicion and doubt.
How could I love you so generously?
And my whole heart continuously give?
How could you take it all with pride
And boldly go on and live?
Letting nothing bother you,
As if you do not even care,
As if you haven't any feeling for me,
Pretending that it isn't there.
How could I love so foolishly?
And freely my heart give,
To someone who knows not of love
And doesn't deserve to live?

So Alone

Dreary Walls,
Silent Night,
Lost Love,
Aching Body,
Longing Heart.
Needy Soul,
Desperate Thoughts.
But, still so alone.
No one,
No one to love me.
No one to hold me in the middle of the night,
No one to rock me into the early morning light,
No one to kiss me down the middle of my back
No one to caress my body giving me the love that I lack.
No one to hold my hand as passionate love is made,
No one kissing my neck with the desire of a love slave,
No one to make me long for more than I need,
No one to partake of an incredibly loving deed.
No one,
No thing,
Oh well.
Roll over,
Go to sleep,
Dream well.

Sorrow

There are times in life
We may not understand,
What exactly is going on,
Or what is in God's plan.
Confused, we accept the situation,
Right then and there,
On our knees we pray to stay,
Within the Lord's tender loving care.
Because we know He will see us through everything.
We review the situation desperately,
Trying for the point to be seen,
Tolerating the loss of a loved one,
Is never an easy task.
It does help when someone asks,
"Is there anything I can do?"
He can't be here now to personally comfort us on earth
So He sends friends to us to extend their loving worth.

Special Reminder

You were given to me as a special reminder,

A gift from the Lord.

You recall to my memory that someone loves me

When times seem hard.

You help me to remember

That regardless who leaves,

You are always here.

You reassure me that through it all

God is constantly near.

Ten little fingers,

Ten little toes,

Two little eyes,

One little nose,

Two little ears,

Two little feet,

Rosy-colored jaws, fluffy and sweet.

Amazingly forgiving of all the off days mothers have,

Always capable of reaching out and bringing about a laugh.

Teaching an unforgettable lesson

About this short and precious life that we live,

Sent as a friendly reminder

There wasn't a better gift that God could give.

Dedicated to my second born son Chorlandrious Raigh Henry

Suicidal Thoughts

Lord, I want to kill myself.
There are so many reasons why
I feel there are no reasons left to live,
Now I want to die.
Not that I'm unappreciative for the life I now live,
Seems like I just can't get right
And do what is your will.
I have been through many changes,
I have been put in a living hell,
I have so much negativity in my life,
My true feelings I can't tell.
When I need to talk—
Because I have a problem or three—
No one wants to take the time
To stop and listen to me.
People don't give me the benefit of the doubt
Because I am fat
I never judge people based on looks,
Clothing or any of that.
Deep inside I know that I am a good person
And indeed true
So why am I always depressed and feeling blue?
I have so much love inside that no one has explored,
Yet and still I feel rejected, unloved, and ignored.
They talk behind my back and tell others
How they perceive me to be,
When they don't know anything
And they don't want me.
I get so confused at times,
I have no clue where to turn,
When someone truthfully loves me,
It takes time for me to learn.
The ones that didn't love me
Left me mentally abused,

The ones that sincerely cared
I sometimes tend to make feel misused.
I do not mean to hurt anyone
Or make anyone cry,
I have so many unresolved issues:
Will they leave if I die?
I know where my future lies,
And what I must do to become the best,
Why, may I ask, does it have to be
Such a frustrating test?

Taking Turns

When it was your turn to let me go
 Into a world unknown,
To let me be who I wanted to be
When into a man I had grown.
When it was your turn,
You let me spread my wings and soar,
You let me go with love
And politely opened the door.
Now, today it is my turn,
But it isn't as easy as it seems,
To let you go into that open door,
And pursue all of your dreams.
Dreams of never hurting again
In body or in soul,
Hopes of an eternal heavenly home—
That was always your goal.
Enjoy your journey home, Mother,
God has seen you through,
I will see you again someday
Until then, remember how much I love you.

Written on behalf of my Godfather for his mother Edna Sharpley

__Thanks for Being my Friend__

Thanks for being my friend
When I needed you the most,
It is to you
I would like to lift a toast.
To a person loyal and true,
Someone identical to you,
Someone to whom my secrets I can tell.
And in your heart I always dwell.
Someone who puts herself last,
It is unto you that I lift this glass.
Thanks for being there
Through the good times, as well as bad,
Thanks for sharing in
The momentous occasions that I've had.
You are truly the one and only of your kind,
I would never disown you as a close personal friend of mine.
I am glad that you are here,
I am glad that your presence is always near.
Thank you for being my friend, so truthful and sincere.

To my cousin Keonie Tanisha Cooper, who was definitely there for me after I lost my mother, letting me know that I had not lost all of my friends.

That it isn't There

I look into your wolf-like eyes
And see your prejudiced stare,
Yet, you want me to believe
That it isn't there.
You slash my intellect with false words,
Pretending that you care,
But when I let you know that I'm not dumb,
You pretend that sarcasm is not there
I'm not black because I choose to be,
Or due to the color of my skin.
I am black because you desire me to be
And have chosen not to see what's within.
You know my capabilities,
Therefore, you try to hold me back,
You treat me like a dark and secret room.
All you see is the color black.
I cook food you consume each day,
With water from the well built by me,
You eat with a merry laugh,
And treat me like black is all I can be.
If ever I stole, I had to,
Because I wasn't given my fair share,
Again you try to make it seem
That it isn't there.
If ever I fought, I was provoked by words
That you knew were untrue,
And there you are again pretending,
And wanting me to do the same thing, too.
The clothes you wear are made from cotton,
Picked and sewn with our hands,
We sweated to lay the railroad tracks,
And connected power to run the fans.
Let's not forget the traffic lights,
Helping to make accidents less,

When ending your day remember,
I made the bed in which you rest.
When I began to rise,
As you never thought I would,
You made sure you did
Every negative thing you could.
You thought you had me beat down,
Well enough to stay,
But the determined soul of a black like me,
Had to be noticed someday.
I am stronger than you imagined
And much more than you will ever be,
It is not that it isn't there,
It is my soul you refuse to see.
I hold no grudge—
God will handle the affair—
When He lets loose,
You won't be able to pretend
That he isn't there!

The Conversation Piece

You came across my mind one day,
You took a seat and stayed.
No matter what I did,
You were in my spirit all the way.
So I went to my secret closet
And talked to God in prayer,
To consult with Him and see
Why this feeling was lingering here.
I called the places I thought you had been,
Then places you could possibly be,
Conversations with family members and friends
Brought a reality check to me,
You had been missing in action for quite a while,
No more could I take.
I was determined to get out and find you,
My business I made it,
With sincere intentions and dedication
Out of the house I set.
The mental image engraved of what I found
I never will forget
Never in all my imagination
Did I think I would see you that way.
Never did I dream when I found you
On the ground you would be laid,
Never did I imagine the last time we spoke
Really was the "last."
Never did I think when I found you
From this life you would've passed,
Some things we have no control over,
Including situations like this,
The life you lived
Is a testimony all your own,

We love you
And
You will be missed.

Written in loving memory of Travis Hines on behalf of Ethel Hines and Family

The Greatest Love of All

The Greatest Love of All,
Besides the love of the Lord and thyself,
Is the love of a mother,
Which brings emotional wealth.
It is the kind of love
That is believed by seeing,
The type of love that is honest, sincere, and pure,
A sweet personality to which every child is lured.
The Greatest gift of all is that special motherly love
Because it is a gift sent from God up above.

The Rose

Love is like a rose,
Sometimes it is opened,
Sometimes it is closed,
Sometimes it withers,
Sometimes it grows.
Sometimes it is given,
Sometimes it is sought,
Sometimes the rain "helps",
Sometimes it needs soil.
Sometimes beautiful results
Make it seem worth the toil.
When the rosebud closes
And the time ends that it can stay,
Precious memories arrive
And grief seems to finally fade.

<u>This Day</u>

This day belongs to an innocent one sent to us
That beautiful day, those years ago,
This day belongs to one that has changed our lives in positive ways
And helped us to grow.
This day belongs to one so exuberant and vivacious
She touches all of our lives with no effort at all,
This day belongs to one that has no untold story,
The way she lives is the picture in the crystal ball.
This day belongs to one that offers a "fairytale" friendship
That seems imaginary yet is real.
This day belongs to one that is always there
And whose honesty you can feel,
This day belongs to a diligent worker
That is good in everything there is for her to do.
This day belongs to one that from the beginning
Has in nature been loyal, pure, and continually true.

This poem was written as a birthday card one year to the lady that is now my former mother-in-law, but who is also the grandmother of my two oldest sons, Mrs. Katherine Myles

Tribute to a Special Great Aunt

Though there are certain things
That happen in life every day,
Some occurrences are hard to accept,
Prepare for them as we may.
When we were created,
We were not intentionally born to die,
So rather than rejoicing in such,
It is our first intuition to cry.
Knowing we will no longer have your laughter,
Nor feel the warmth of your smile,
Being able to recall special moments,
Shared as far back as being a child.
A special reassurance comes
In each ray of glowing sun,
And in the rain-filled flowers
That express your love in each one.
Seeing these natural beauties
Makes it easier to be glad,
We are thankful to Jesus
For the Blessed and unforgotten time that we had.

Poem written in dedication to my late Great Aunt Bernice Wesley Richardson, with love

__Tribute to the Mother I Knew__

I know deep within my heart and soul

That God does no wrong,

I am very grateful to Him

That you did not have to suffer long.

You have fulfilled your earthly duties,

They are all finished, done, and through,

Since we did not talk one last time

I thought I'd say right now

How much I loved you.

It is not going to be easy,

But, very hard at first,

This seems like death to us,

Really it is your birth.

The things you spoke of and wanted me to do,

Just because your soul is resting,

Does not mean I will disappoint you.

All of your earthly duties are finished, done, and through,

A dutiful Mother and trustworthy friend were you!

I LOVE YOU

This poem was written as a loving tribute in memory of Mrs. Corine Wesley Taylor,
my Great Aunt/Foster Mother

You are Life

As the morning sun awakens us
And I look into your eyes,
As the evening moonlight cradles us
While I rock away your cries,
As I gently stroke your cheeks
And look upon your face,
As I lay you upon a bed of rest
With a kind and gentle grace.
As you go through each day,
Trusting me to care for you as you do.
As you return a stare into my eyes,
Hinting that your love for me is true,
As you were given to me temporarily
To make life more worthwhile,
Precious moments like these
Bring me to an appreciation for you, my child.
You are life.
You are what it is about.
Now that I have been blessed with your presence
I can not imagine going without.

Written in dedication to my fourth born son Keon Jayverick Deshawn Earl

About the Author

Photograph was taken by Shaw's Photography of Monroe, La.

Adesha Letrise Madison was born on January 22, 1976 to Ms. Ruby Lee Madison (deceased) and Mr. Prentiss Lee Square. She was adopted by her biological Aunt and Uncle, Corine and Eddie Taylor, and was reared by both until the age of 14, then continued the rest of her youth into adulthood being reared by her father Eddie Taylor, or "Paw Paw," as he is called. She became Mrs. Adesha Letrise Madison-Earl August 2006. She is the proud mother of four boys: Clifton Daljuan Xavier Henry, Chorlandrious Raigh Henry, (from her 1st marriage), and Christopher Edward Reese Earl, and Keon Jayverick Deshawn Earl, from the present marriage. She is a native of West Monroe, Louisiana, resided in Toledo, Ohio, 2006-2009, and is now back in Louisiana. Adesha has an Associates in Office Management, and recently acquired her Associates in Paralegal. Writing has been a life-long passion for her and she hopes to continue writing poetry, pursue writing children's books, fiction, and hopefully an autobiography. She hopes to reach audiences of all ages and interests. Her major poetic influences were Maya Angelou, Gwendolyn Brooks, and Langston Hughes, but she hopes to bring something special to the forefront as a unique individual with her own style.

<u>The Virgin Man</u>

If I had met a virgin man.

One who has never held my hand,

One who has never walked my "land,"

One who has never kissed my lips,

One who has never caressed my hips,

One who has never felt my stride,

One who has never been inside,

Inside my hopes,

Inside my dreams,

Inside my heart, my inner being.

Inside my soul,

Inside my head,

And never been inside my bed.

The virgin man, himself untouched,

Starting a life that means so much,

So much to him, so much to me,

Being all we both can be,

Being loving,

Being caring,

Showing compassion,

Always sharing,

Sharing Joy,

And

Sharing Pain,

Sharing Sunshine,

Sharing Rain,

Sharing Passion,

Sharing Pride,

No one could our love divide.

Oh, yes the virgin man,

One who would romance me again and again.

Oh to him I would have given,

My virginity and passion I'd hidden

Hidden under my clothes

Hidden deep down within my soul

Hidden beneath my skin
Oh, yes I would sin
Sin with the virgin man
And repent over and over again.

<u>By: Adesha L. Madison</u>

If you enjoyed this poem, you will enjoy the author's next book Poetic Transitions (Fall) The 2nd of a 4 Part Series. Coming Soon!!!!